The Secret in Morris Valley

By Linda (NMI) Joy

© 2014 by Trudy V Myers

Printed in December 2021
10 9 8 7 6 5 4 3 2 1

MoonPhaze LLC, 613 del Pilar Dr., Groveland FL, 34736
MoonPhaze.com

Cover Design: SelfPubBookCovers.com/FrinaArt

The Secret in Morris Valley

By Linda (NMI) Joy

The Secret in Morris Valley

In order to fly, she'd had to pack the guns in her suitcases, but she didn't expect she'd need them before she unpacked. She suspected Dr Jadlowski was overly concerned, and his weapons would be completely unnecessary. Danger seemed so very far away.

The car's seats were wickedly comfortable, one might say luxurious. The heater kept the temperature at summer evening balmy, a counterpoint to the muddy, half-melted snow banks at the road's edge. The engine purred so quietly, it might have been a contented kitten.

"We're nearly there, Miss." Fredrick, the chauffeur, had been friendly when he picked her up at the airport, but not talkative. That was alright with Ondrea. She was too overwhelmed to pay attention to mindless chatter.

They had left the city behind, passed meadows of grazing sheep and cows, fields being prepared for crops. Looking ahead, she saw a forest coating the mountains they approached. To the left, a river flanked the road, headed in the other direction.

Ondrea settled deeper into the seat and stared out the car window. Trees held naked branches up, reaching for the sky, like robbery victims. The thin twigs did nothing to eclipse the weak winter sun, but their silhouettes traced a black spider web against the pale sky.

The car slowed to cross a bridge. The water looked cold, and swift, with white wavelets that resembled chunks of ice.

Leaving the winter sight behind, the vehicle started a climb so steep, it felt like a 45-degree slope. Ridiculous thought, of course, but nerve-wracking, just the same. Ondrea made herself small in the back seat and trusted the driver to keep the car's tires on the road.

A few minutes later, Ondrea glimpsed a house through the trees. Stone walls, slate roof, and arched windows gave an impression of age and stability. The forest abruptly ended, and the car pulled around the center of a circular drive, came to a smooth halt.

Broad steps led to a pair of recessed doors overlooked by windows and a deep overhang. Those doors probably never saw sunlight, except possibly at dawn.

The house continued to either side, three stories tall, with a dozen windows on each floor in each direction. A mansion built generations ago, meant to last.

The ground floor windows had bars. This was a fortress, standing firm against the world.

Fredrick had already stepped around the car to open her door. Ondrea shrugged on her worn cloth coat, and stepped out onto the bricks. still damp and slippery with early spring frost.

Fredrick got her luggage from the trunk. Ondrea hesitated at the bottom step uncertainly. She supposed she had come more as an employee than a guest. Should she go to the servants' entrance? Did people still think in terms of servants' entrances?

The huge doors opened, and a butler started down the stairs. Before he traversed half a dozen steps, a pack of huge dogs burst from the trees and raced forward, teeth bared.

At the sound of snarls and growls, the sight of huge animals bearing down on her, Ondrea cringed against the car, her heart racing. Dogs ran forward as one mass, uncontrolled and uncontrollable, intent on tearing her into tiny pieces. Her heartbeat came to a premature end.

A shrill whistle pierced the animals' noise, the crisp air, and Ondrea's ear drums. The dogs roiled to a stop in the driveway, still growling, still anxious to get their fangs into her soft body. But something, someone was keeping them back.

Men emerged from the trees. The leader of the human pack was tall and muscular, ruggedly handsome. As he strode forward, he issued another shrill whistle. The dogs' snarls and growls faded, some became whimpers. Canine spines curled, paws lifted and posteriors lowered nervously, up and down, up and down.

Still huddled against the car, Ondres closed her eyes and covered her ears. "Stop it, stop it," she chanted quietly. Her legs shook, and her lungs were too compressed to work properly.

Strong hands took hold of her wrists. She was gently pulled upright. When her eyes fluttered open, she found the lead man standing before her, his blue eyes staring down at her intently. "No need to fear my dogs. Not when I'm here."

She glanced past him, to where the human pack slipped leashes on the canines, who waited calmly, watching her, but no longer threatening. "I don't—I've never liked dogs."

He let go of her. "And my dogs don't like much of anybody. But they follow orders." He stepped back and turned to the chauffeur. "Take her luggage to the Blue Room, Fredrick."

"Yes, sir."

The human handlers led the dogs away. The animals went, but not without backward glances, the occasional rumble in their throats.

The dogs forgotten, the tall man asked, "You are Ms El Lobos?" He pronounced her name with a Spanish flair, as two words. El lobos. *The wolves*.

"Yes," she agreed. "Ondrea Ellobos." She pronounced it the way she was used to hearing it; all slammed together, a slight accent on the first syllable. "Thank you for sending your car for me, Mr Morris." She offered her hand. He shook it briefly before pulling his away.

"Safest way to get you here," he said, and turned to the butler. "Tarver, show Ms El Lobos to the Blue Room. She still has two hours before dinner."

He turned back to her. "The house is large, and it's easy to become disoriented when you're new. For a few days, please call a servant, who will take you wherever you wish to go." He pulled his lips into a thin smile. "The neighbor's wife was lost for hours on her first visit."

"I understand." *No house is that complex*. "Mr Morris, there may be some misunderstanding. My name isn't Spanish. It isn't even mine, really. I'm a foundling, and they had to put something on the paperwork."

" 'A rose by any other name—'," he quoted, but otherwise paid little attention to her protest. "After dinner, we'll discuss the reason why you're here."

That surprised her. She had been sent as a research botanist by Dr Jadlowski, her favorite instructor at the University. She tried not to frown in confusion. A library had been mentioned, too. Perhaps they should discuss her assignment, after all.

"I believe the stairs are dry, if you would step forward, Miss." Ondrea stared at the hand offered her. It was masculine, but old. She raised her gaze to the butler, who waited patiently.

Mr Morris had turned away, already bored. His men and dogs were still in sight. Morris' attention alternated between the dogs and the forest line, a hundred yards away.

Ondrea took the butler's hand lightly, though she didn't need his help, and stepped from damp cobblestones to dry stairs. "Thank you," she said, letting go. His hand swept toward the doors, and she prepared to step forward.

"Ms El Lobos."

He still pronounced it wrong, but she turned, never-the-less. "Yes, Mr Morris?"

"It's best I get this said right away, so you know what your limitations are. Don't leave the house between dusk and dawn. Don't leave the house during the day without a male escort. And no matter what, don't enter the forest."

Ondrea had never tolerated chauvinistic treatment well, but she kept her temper under control and her voice mild. "Are you afraid I might get lost, Mr Morris?"

"No, I'm afraid you might get killed," he answered. "This forest is filled with wild creatures. Dangerous creatures, who have no respect or fear of mankind. My dogs do the best they can, but they can't protect you if you wander into the forest."

Considering how little dogs liked her, she felt it more likely the dogs would kill her themselves, if their master wasn't there to control them. "I see." He gave a short nod and moved off. Ondrea started up the broad staircase.

The foyer had an inlaid floor of pale and dark wood, richly polished. Tarver led her up the left side of the curving double staircase. The second floor landing was covered in thick carpet with a geometric pattern that looked vaguely American Indian.

The turned into the south wing, and traveled down the hall for some distance before the butler opened a door on the left. "The Blue Room, Miss Ellobos," he intoned.

He got her name right. Why couldn't his employer?"

They stepped into a spacious room with pale blue walls. The furniture was of dark wood, appropriate pieces upholstered in cream fabric with blue flowers. The drapes were a luxurious blue, with cream accents. The fireplace was faced in white marble with faint blue veins.

Stunned by the elegance, Ondrea hadn't even begun to wonder where anything was located before Tarver stated, "The bedroom, closet and bathroom are through that door, Miss. Wilma is unpacking your bags, and would be happy to draw a bath, should you desire one."

She swallowed her surprise at having the services of a maid, the use of a suite, rather than a simple bedroom. The house was huge, and no doubt empty of guests, so Morris could be generous. However, a gilded cage was still a cage. "Thank you, Tarver. I'll consider that."

"Dinner is served at six. When you are ready, Wilma will show you to the dining room."

Another of Lord Morris' restrictions. Ondrea winced to realize she had already started thinking of him as 'Lord'. This assignment might not be as easy as she had thought, if he continued to irritate her.

But she didn't know where the dining room was, so having a guide might ensure she arrived on time. "Thank you," she said again. The butler bowed and turned to the door.

A terrifying thought occurred to her, and she turned quickly to catch the man before he left. "Tarver, am I expected to dress for dinner?"

His eyes twinkled. "Nudity would be best left in your room, Miss."

She smiled. "I was afraid Mr Morris might expect elegant gowns, which I don't have."

"The housekeeper is lucky if he cleaned the mud from his boots, most evenings," the butler replied dryly, and left.

So she didn't need to worry much about her wardrobe. On the other hand, she wasn't looking forward to sharing meals with the lord of the manor. Perhaps it would only be this once.

* * *

In such a grand house, Ondrea expected a grand dining hall, with a table large enough to seat dozens, sideboards along the walls, and a marble floor. Instead, Wilma led her to a small and cozy room, with a round table with four chairs, a buffet, and heavy drapes along a wall.

There were 3 settings on the table, so she wouldn't be dining alone with the lord—with Mr Morris. Wilma left her alone in the room.

The middle-aged maid had efficiently unpacked Ondrea's suitcases, placing clothes in drawers and closet, and toiletries on the bathroom counter. She had left the handgun and ammunition in plain sight on the bed, with a calm, "I wasn't sure where you would want those, Miss." As if every guest to this house came armed.

Ondrea studied the two small portraits over the buffet—uninspired likenesses in suits from long ago. Both men bore a resemblance to Mr Morris. Two of his ancestors, no doubt.

Bored with those, she peeked behind the drapes, and found French doors that looked out into a garden. It was already dark, so she couldn't see much, but the paths and stone benches made it plain she was looking at a garden.

"I suggest you close the drapes before Barry arrives," said a deep voice.

Surprised, she turned to the newcomer. His blond hair was longish, his eyes brown, and his skin well tanned, even at winter's end. He wore both a turtleneck sweater and a plaid flannel shirt, with corduroy pants and heavy work boots. He had tried to scrape the boots free of mud.

She didn't remember seeing him in Morris' human pack. Ondrea stepped away from the French doors, let the drapes fall into

6

their accustomed place. "Hello."

The blond crossed the room to take her hand. He smiled at her for a long moment. "Welcome to Morris Lodge, Miss El Lobos. "I'm Ralph Cooney, the foreman." His aftershave was earthy and musky, his hand hot and calloused.

"Good evening." She tugged her hand free. "I'm afraid there's a misconception about my name. It is not El Lobos, it is Ellobos. I tried to explain that to Mr Morris this afternoon."

"You'd best resign yourself to El Lobos," he advised. "He's obsessed with wolves."

"Surely it's not an obsession yet," came a dry rejoinder. "Although, I will admit a fascination with them." Morris smoothed his sport coat, as if he had just put it on as he stepped into the room. "But that's understandable, since this valley has so many of them. They do represent a considerable danger."

"I don't agree they're any bigger a problem here than any other place," Cooney returned.

"Not this argument again," Morris said as he pulled the bell cord near the doorway, two sharp tugs. "It is Ms El Lobos' first meal with us, and I would prefer to make a better impression than that." He pulled a chair out from the table. "Would you care to sit here, Ms El Lobos? I prefer to face the drapes."

"He's afraid the wolves will come through the glass," Cooney revealed.

Morris' voice was several degrees colder. "I asked you to drop the subject, Ralph."

"As you wish," Cooney gave in. Ondrea could almost hear the whine in his voice, like a whipped cur admitting defeat. "Would you like some wine with dinner, Miss Ellobos?"

"I have no tolerance for alcohol, even wine. So no, thank you." She slipped into the chair Morris still held for her.

Morris had a white turtleneck under his brown sport coat, with new jeans and black athletic shoes that looked fresh from the store. Not a speck of mud or dust on him.

As Morris slid her chair closer to the table, a faint scent of spices beguiled her nose. For one fleeting millisecond, she regretted her choice of attire. Her blouse buttoned up to her neck, so it allowed him absolutely no glimpse of cleavage. As she realized what she was thinking, she blushed. She hoped no one noticed.

"How was your journey, Ms El Lobos?" Morris asked as he sat down facing the French doors. "Uneventful, I hope."

Ondrea was on the verge of saying, 'lavish'. She had planned to drive from the state university to Morris Point. When the mail had brought an airline ticket, she had been nonplussed. "You certainly were generous in your arrangements, Mr Morris," she stated, choosing her words carefully.

"Was I?"

"I would have been happy to drive."

Wilma arrived to set salads on the table, along with rolls and ice water.

"Wilma, what has cook made this evening?" Cooney asked.

"Chicken cordon bleu, asparagus tips and twice baked potatoes."

"Wonderful!" Cooney sat at the table. "I made a tour of the east slope field, Barry."

Morris held up a hand to stop him. "I know we've habitually discussed business at the dinner table, Cooney, but we didn't have anyone else here. Let's start the workday with a business meeting, and not bore Ms El Lobos."

"You're the boss," Cooney agreed, and started his salad.

Morris turned. "To return to our conversation, Ms El Lobos, Dr Jadlowski wasn't sure your vehicle would get you here. Traveling alone isn't safe for a woman. If you had managed to get to this valley before your car broke down, I am 99% certain you would not have survived."

"My car isn't that bad," she protested.

"Perhaps not. I only had Dr Jadlowski's opinion to go by. I considered sending Fredrick to the capital to pick you up, but Ralph convinced me an airline ticket would be adequate."

"Adequate!" She sipped her water, tried to compose herself. "Mr Morris, a first class seat was far more than 'adequate'!"

"First class," he repeated softly, and studied the smile Cooney couldn't quite keep off his face. "Yes, one might think that generous." He dismissed the subject. "How is Dr Jadlowski? Still a cantankerous old crack-pot?"

His attitude startled her. "Mr Morris, I thought you used to be one of his best pupils."

"Once upon a time. As you are now." He smiled. "Only his best students get to call him both cantankerous and a crack-pot."

"I wouldn't know."

Morris ate a bite of salad thoughtfully. "Doc told me about your study skills, Ms El Lobos, but no information on you as a person. Apparently, he didn't feel it important. Or perhaps he hadn't bothered to learn anything about you. But I hope you'll indulge my curiosity."

"I've been putting myself through college by working at the library. And now Dr Jad got me this study to do."

He looked ready to frown. "I meant to ask about your family, your home, and so on."

"There isn't much. I'm an orphan, raised by a couple with their family, rather than made a ward of the state. I'm not sure how they did it; perhaps they used their daughter's birth certificate, forged my name onto it. Rather, the name they'd given me, I guess."

She set aside her fork, the salad finished. "To others, they claimed I was their ward; but they told me they'd found me beside the road. I can't complain. They did their best for me."

She sipped her water, ready to stop, but he apparently expected her to go on. "I don't know anything about my biological family, but my adoptive family consists of parents, two brothers, and three sisters. And what about you two, your families?"

"Oh, there's Cooneys all over this valley," Cooney stated. "They don't all use the name." Meaning his sisters had married, she assumed. But that usually went without saying.

Tarver entered and replaced empty salad plates with plates of hot food. "Dessert is apple pie a la mode," he revealed. "Will you need anything else before that, sir?"

Morris glanced around the table. "I don't believe so. Thank you, Tarver."

After the butler left, he answered Ondrea's question. "Shortly after the Louisiana Purchase, our families settled in this valley. They raised livestock on the south end, and farmed the north end. The Morris' never sold any of the land, although some bits and pieces have been leased, allowing employees to have homes and businesses."

He owned the entire valley? She had seen it from the airplane; it was huge!

"As for my immediate family, my mother died when I was six, giving birth to my sister. My father hired a wet nurse, a woman passing through, who gave birth the same night. After three years, that family disappeared. Along with my sister." He took a bite of his entree.

Confused by the man's dry recitation, Ondrea looked to Cooney. The foreman shrugged one shoulder, but his brown eyes stared at her intently. That didn't tell her anything, either.

Morris continued. "For many years, Dad and I were alone. Then I suddenly had a stepmother." He took a bite of potato.

"That must have been strange," Ondrea said. She wondered how old he'd been when the new mother had entered his life.

"It was awkward," he said. "Since I'd dated her in high school. And she hadn't changed. So I went to college. Got me out of the house, for the most part. I thought Dad could handle things here on his own. He said he could."

"And he did," Ralph stated. "Until he died."

"Oh, no!" It slipped out. She had been fairly certain there was no elder Mr Morris. Cooney was heartless, to be so flippant. She wondered where the stepmother was. Traveling in Europe, living high off the Morris bankroll?

Morris glared at Cooney. "I won't bore you with details, Ms El Lobos. I don't have many, since I was at school when it happened. My stepmother went out one evening. My father went after her. They were found in the woods. What the wolves had left of them."

"How terrible!" How could he remain so bland about it?

"Perhaps now you can understand why I have such Draconian rules for those who live here. I'm trying to keep people alive."

"Barry was traumatized by the loss of his father and

stepmother," Cooney stated. "Almost as much as he was to find Karen was his new step-mom. Back in high school—"

"How is your chicken, Ralph?" Morris interrupted. "I know you prefer your meat still pink in the middle, but cook doesn't allow that with chicken."

"Yes," Cooney agreed with a frown. "She and I have discussed this many times." He didn't answer Morris' question, but he took the hint and didn't return to tales of high school.

The remaining meal time was spent in lighter conversation concerning the weather and current events in the wider world. Mostly, it centered on celebrity scandals, as if Morris wasn't sure of her intellect. Not an unusual reaction to her, unfortunately. For the millionth time, she wondered if it was her blond hair.

* * *

When supper drew to a close, Tarver and Wilma arrived to clear the table. Ondrea started to speak, but Morris beat her. "Tarver, compliments to your wife on a splendid meal, as always."

"Thank you, sir. She was hoping to please the young lady."

Here was her chance to express herself. "It was marvelous! I shall gain ten pounds!"

"Maybe Barry will let you use his exercise room," Cooney suggested. Morris, however, did not immediately make that offer, so the suggestion faded into uneasy silence. As Cooney pulled Ondrea's chair back so she could stand, he leaned close to whisper, "Or you and I could give each other a workout."

She stepped away, sure she knew what he meant. She'd heard similar suggestions before.

"Ms El Lobos, perhaps I should show you your office," Morris suggested.

"Yes," she agreed readily. "That would be nice."

"Cooney, don't forget our business meeting in the morning."

"I'll be there," the foreman promised.

Morris was quiet while they walked. When they crossed the central hall, Ondrea said, "You have an interesting relationship

11

with your foreman. If you don't mind my saying."

After several steps, Morris replied. "There is an old saying, I don't remember who said it. But the advice is to keep your friends close."

The end of that is that you should keep your enemies even closer."

"How interesting," he stated blandly. Ondrea wondered how much of that saying he'd already known, whether it implied Cooney was a close friend, or an enemy. Why would anyone keep an enemy on the payroll? He must be extremely good at whatever foremen do.

"Do you remember my rules, about having a male escort if you go outside?"

"It's only been a few hours since you told me, Mr Morris."

"Barry," he said softly. "I don't recommend that Cooney be your escort. There's more than one type of wolf in this valley."

"I understand."

"I doubt it." He opened a pair of doors on the left. A flick of the lights, and they entered a huge room. Bookshelves lined every wall, except for the fireplace and two windows, currently covered by drapes. The room's second floor balcony gave access to the upper reaches. In addition, each sofa and easy chair had a small bookcase butted up behind it.

"The library," Morris explained unnecessarily. "I think you'll find all the reference material you need. Left of the fireplace are all the diaries written since this valley was settled."

"All?" The number of journals implied not all had been written by family members.

He nodded. "You'll find references to the Morris Valley Wolf in those. The right side holds the formal papers; birth and death certificates, arrests, judgments, and so forth, gathered together and called Legal Logs. A much drier source, but the Wolves are mentioned."

"That's a lot of reading to do," she observed.

Morris grimaced. "I was about to say you can explore the rest of the books at will, should you want some reading material."

"Thank you. However, I tend to get caught up in my work."

"So I've heard."

He crossed to the shelves next to the fireplace and pulled on a pair of handles attached to the upright supports. Shelves swung open, revealing darkness beyond.

While thoughts of hidden passages raced through Ondrea's mind, Morris reached around the edge. Lights came on, revealing a smaller room, also lined with bookshelves, mostly empty.

"Your office." He gestured her inside.

A desk sat in the middle of the polished wooden floor, with all the usual desk accoutrements. A normal door to the hallway was opposite the bank of drapes. A second desk in one corner held a computer. Two chairs upholstered in red damask faced the main desk.

Morris sat in one of those chairs, and, since he seemed to expect it, Ondrea took the other. "Now," he began, "Doc charged me with seeing to your well-being while you're here. Warned me you get completely involved in your work, and forget to eat or sleep."

"Like he has room to talk," she muttered.

"I never understood that much commitment, so here are the rules."

"Rules!" Who did he think he was?

He ignored her outburst. "I expect you to work roughly forty hours a week. I don't care when, except I do expect you to join me—us—for dinner at six each evening, properly attired. Breakfast is served between six and eight, lunch between eleven and two. If you prefer not to interrupt your work, you can use the intercom to request refreshments be brought here." He pointed to the phone on the desk. "But not dinner."

He was acting like her father! Or something. She was a grown woman, capable of taking care of herself! But for the sake of this study, she'd put up with his stupid rules. She felt her mouth tighten. "Exactly what do you expect me to wear to dinner?" she asked.

He stared at her for a long moment. His face may have reddened slightly, but she wasn't sure. "I don't consider swimsuits, shorts or halters to be proper attire for a meal."

"Fine," she agreed. She hadn't brought most of those. And if she had, she wouldn't be inclined to wear them in late winter, in a house where at least one 'human wolf' resided. "I will do my best to curb my enthusiasm for my work and only work forty hours a week."

"Good." He studied her a moment, made a decision. "I know that you're doing this study for Dr Jadlowski, but the pay isn't good. You took it, though it meant taking a semester away from your studies, because you didn't have the money to continue your studies anyway."

"Dr Jad told you an awful lot about me."

"Brilliant men are not always smart. I'd like to offer you a second job, one you can do at the same time as the study of Morris Valley Wolves, using the same references."

Her first thought was that there was more than one human wolf in the house. But the more he talked, the less it sounded like a proposition. "What would you expect me to do?"

"Find me a wife."

Ondrea's mouth fell open. She made an effort to close it again. "What?"

"I'm not getting any younger. It's time I have children."

"Why do you need help? You're a handsome man. Surely any number of the locals—"

"Are my cousins," he interrupted, and she stared at him in confusion. "Everyone here is descended from the original settlers. All the families have intermarried, including mine."

He crossed his legs. "I tried to figure which were the least related to me, but it was too confusing for the limited time I could devote to it. So I leave it to you to compile a list of eligible women, ranked by how little they are related to me."

Her mind whirled with the enormity of the project he proposed, so she tried to pin down details. "What do you consider marriageable age?"

He grimaced. "Since the intention is to have children, no more than thirty. No younger than eighteen, to avoid charges of pedophilia."

She shoved that ugly thought away, shook her head. "I

wouldn't know where to begin."

"With the diaries and records in the library," he stated dryly, and stood. "Just take notes as you read for the Doc's study, construct a family tree for the valley as best you can. That should be enough to answer my question."

She sighed and stood up also. "I envision one big family tree. It starts with several trunks, but the branches have all merged, divided, and merged, over and over again."

"Exactly," he agreed. "Doc said you were a whiz at breaking down the most complex problems into manageable tasks. This office and everything in it is at your disposal, as is the library. If you need something else, let me know."

"I—I need to think," she stammered.

"Certainly." He glanced at his watch. "I've got some work to do in my own office, but let me first show you to your room." He opened the door to the hall.

"I can find it." As he gazed at her uncertainly, she added, "I have been there before, and the house's layout isn't complicated. Besides, if I get lost, all I have to do is enter a room and pull the bell cord to summon a rescuer, right?"

He smiled and they stepped into the hallway. He turned off the light in 'her' office and opened the opposing door.

"Then I bid you good evening, Ms El Lobos. Feel free to call on the servants for anything you might want." He flicked on the light in the new room, revealing an office much like hers, with a stack of papers on the desk.

"Good night, Mr Morris," she returned, and started up the corridor.

* * *

The light was already on in her sitting room. Ralph Cooney looked up and used a remote to turn off the television. She hadn't realized that dresser held a color television.

"Mr Cooney." She kept her voice cold as she stood in the doorway. "I'm not accustomed to finding men in my room."

15

He smiled as he slowly stood. "We could change that."

"I don't believe so."

The smile didn't falter. "Or I could start finding you in my room."

He had an enticing smiles. She wondered what his kiss would be like, imagined herself pressed against him in passion. He was a human wolf. That's what Morris had implied. She hadn't liked him at dinner. If she was going to dream of being pressed against a man, why not Morris? No, what was she thinking? She had no business dreaming about any man. "That, neither," she returned firmly.

Once she actually got started with her work, she wouldn't have to worry about dreaming of men. She really did get lost in her work.

Cooney started forward, as if he expected her to melt into his arms. She made a mental decision how close she'd let him get before she stepped away. She wouldn't let him get within reach. That would only complicate things.

"We're a long way from town, Ondrea. Entertainment possibilities out here are limited, at best. You should think things over before you dismiss any options."

"I don't consider sex to be mere entertainment."

He paused for a deep breath. "Don't dismiss my offer lightly, girl. You'll need someone to go with you if you want to take a walk, explore the gardens, or even sit in the sunshine."

"There are other men in this household."

"They have work to do. And if you're expecting to strike up a friendship with Barry, save your time. He thinks you're his long-lost sister."

That caught her by surprise. "What?"

"He's never given up on finding her. He's almost as obsessive about that as the wolves. You fit the bill. You were 'found' about the same time his sister disappeared. You were raised by Mexicans, like his sister's wet-nurse. He's pretty sure you're his sister."

Ondrea's mind veered to Ralph's physical attributes again. She shook her head in dismay, took another step away.

Cooney went on. "He might accept you as a sister. But you'd be married off to one of the locals to cement some strained relationship or another."

"I'm not his sister," she told him tartly. "Leave my room."

She had backed into and down the hall, to keep as much distance as possible between them. After a moment, Cooney sauntered out. "Ponder this, sweetheart. If he didn't think you were his sister, why send you a first-class ticket?" He turned and headed for the main staircase.

Ondrea sighed and entered her room. The nerve of some men! And, based on her reaction—even though she didn't like him—Cooney was used to getting his way with women.

She stepped inside and closed the door. Cooney had raised a good question. There really was no reason to have sent her an airline ticket, let alone a first-class one. So—

Her mind cleared, like a mist-shrouded field in the full light of the sun. She felt her tension melt away. Actually, she'd had the impression Morris hadn't actually sent that ticket. Or if he had, some misunderstanding had made it first-class instead of coach. She shouldn't attach too much importance to it.

She shoved the whole question aside. She liked solving problems, and Morris had just handed her one that he was willing to pay her to solve.

If he was too busy to spend more than one meal a day with her, that suited her; she wasn't big on mixing socially with employers. Or co-workers, so she hoped Cooney had gotten the message, though his type seldom did.

She might be spending a lot of time in this room. Thankfully, the 'dresser' held a color TV, a video player and several videos. If she was a bird in a cage—in another cage—then at least she wouldn't die of boredom. She got her exercise videos to work off the day's tension.

*   *   *

After an early breakfast, Ondrea headed for her office. As she turned the door handle, she was startled by a muffled thud behind her, followed by a raised voice.

"I don't care that you sent a first-class ticket! The cost is insignificant! She's here at my invitation, and it is my money, so don't try to tell me how to spend it! It's not your business!"

Cooney's response was a hint of noise through the closed door. She didn't want to listen, and was in such a hurry, her door closed more loudly behind her than she expected. She settled her nerves by turning on the computer, to find out what programs she had to work with.

Several minutes later, she looked around when her office door opened. Morris glanced at his watch. "Don't you want breakfast first?"

"I've had breakfast," she responded. "Thank you."

"I see. Well, I'll let you work, then." He closed the door much more softly than she had managed. Perhaps he didn't realize his argument with Cooney had been overheard.

If Cooney thought he had a say in how Morris spent money, it could be a source of tension in the house. That would be wonderful, to live in a house with that much tension. She'd do the job as quickly as she could, and hopefully would be back at the university by summer.

*   *   *

From the diary of Dalton Morris, September 9, 1824:

We have been here for so long without our wives, only ourselves to keep each other company, and that has long since worn thin. The men have succumbed to use of the farm animals, in an effort to find relief. I fear if word of this practice ever reached the ears of civilization, we would all be burned at the stake as practitioners of witchcraft.

Noah Silas in the worst. While the rest do it in the heat of the moment, they are shamed by it. But Noah's

18

brags of his 'conquests' become more outlandish each day. Today, he claimed to have seduced a wolf, multiple times. Since he is still alive, unharmed, it's impossible, of course, but hard to listen to.

What is this valley doing to us?

Ondrea read the passage again. That was pretty plain talking, considering when it was written. She agreed with him. A man having sex with a wolf would never happen. Noah Silas obviously had quite a lot imagination.

From the diary of Dalton Morris, October 11, 1824:

Silas returned from hunting today. He brought no food, only another mouth to feed; a squad he purchased. She did not seem happy with her circumstances, her feet hobbled and her hands tied, but that is the way of these people; pay the dowry, and you may have the woman.

Silas took great pleasure in describing her charms. He did not, however, offer to share her; and God help me, I am of two minds over that. One, it breeds discontent, that Silas has what they do not. Two, it is unforgivable that any of us would use a woman against her will.

Tomorrow, Ed Long and Upton Brown head east, before winter makes the passes impossible. They will gather our families, and return in the spring.

The more Ondrea read about Noah Silas, the less she liked him. All the men had undergone the same hardships, yet he had apparently reverted to barbarism, keeping a woman tied up and making 'use' of her to suit his needs! Obviously, the first Mr Morris had a hard time keeping his settlement from completely degenerating.

From the Legal Log, 1821 to 1825:

October 11, 1824 - Noah Silas has returned to the valley with a wife, Young Fawn, apparently of the

Kotamwa tribe, or possibly a tribe further away.

* * *

The day had been dark and dreary. The weather was gathering strength for one last snowstorm, which would, no doubt, be horrific.

Ondrea had the habit of opening her office drapes each morning, to take advantage of the natural light. Mr Morris closed them each afternoon when he came to remind her that it was nearly time for dinner. Today, open drapes hadn't been enough, and the room's lights were on, too, as Ondrea delved deeper into the generations of this valley.

From the Legal Log, 1821 to 1825:

August 30, 1825 - Our population has nearly quadrupled with the arrival of wives and children.

There followed a list of women's names, each the 'wife of' an original settler, and followed by the names of children they brought with them.

There was no wife listed for Noah Silas. In a diary entry dated a few days before, Morris had commented that Young Fawn was large with child, but Silas still kept her fettered.

And still no mention of the Morris Valley Wolves she had come to study.

She left the comfortable chair for the computer to start the 'family tree' she'd promised.

She paused as a distant howl invaded the room. A wolf. Perhaps the day's dimness had confused it. It was far away, more than a mile, she would guess. One of the Morris Valley Wolves? Or just a wolf? Impossible to tell from the voice, at an unknown distance.

Dr Jad had been sure the wolves were odd in this valley. Perhaps he'd listened to Mr Morris too much. Dismissing the wolves, she began constructing a genealogical database.

Ondrea was startled by another howl, much louder, closer, only yards from the house, it seemed. The dogs barked, but their din was more remote than the latest howl. Her heart pounding, Ondrea crossed the room to stare out the window. It was getting dark already, or maybe the fog made it seem so, since one couldn't see far.

The wolf who had sounded so close could be in those bushes. Would a wolf come that close? Why? She shuddered and pulled the drapes closed, thankful for the bars on the windows.

When the door opened, she whirled, her heart thudding. Morris stared at her from the doorway and the strain in his face relaxed. "I was afraid you'd gone out."

"That's against your rules," she pointed out. "Without a male."

"Well, I didn't know. All the staff is inside, except Cooney. I thought maybe—"

"That would be against your advice," she stated. *And against my better judgment.*

He glanced at the computer, which was obviously on, and the open book on the desk, the notes she'd been making. "Have you had lunch?"

"Not yet." She returned to her desk, pulled the journal close to resume her work.

"If you had lunch with me, we could take a walk in the garden afterwards," he suggested. "There isn't much to see, given the season and the weather, but it's outside. Once the storm begins, a walk might not be possible for several days."

It didn't take her long to decide. It was a big house, and she had barely seen any of it, so far, but if the weather was going to turn bad, she should get outside while she could. She set the log aside. "Thank you. That's very generous."

As she stood up, however, Morris closed the door. "I neglected to mention, Ms El Lobos, that I'd prefer you not tell anyone that I've hired you. Or why."

"I haven't had any opportunity. But if anybody should ask— which seems unlikely—I could simply say I'm constructing a valley-wide family tree, which is true, out of curiosity. What's done with the information isn't anybody's business."

"There are those who wouldn't agree," he stated and stared at her for a long moment. His hand was still on the door handle, but he made no move to open it.

Uneasy, Ondrea cleared her throat. "I'm not in the habit of making suggestions that would put me out of a job. However, there is an easier way to find what you want to know."

"Is there?"

Was he out of touch with the world? She thought ranchers and breeders were always looking for a way to improve their stock. "DNA," she stated. "Genetics. Just line all the ladies up, get a sample of their DNA, and let the lab figure out which is the least related to you."

He looked startled, then embarrassed. "I thought of that. I made inquiries, tried to figure out how to do it. But it seems unlikely it would work. We aren't talking steers, after all."

"You seem cold-blooded about finding the love of your life." She clamped her mouth shut, appalled by her words.

One corner of his mouth rose a millimeter. "Yes, it must seem that way. Anyway, to collect a DNA sample from people, you must explain why you want it. And the fact is, there is a—" He shifted his weight uneasily. "A condition, an illness, in this valley. "Not everyone is... infected. Not even whole families. I have no reason to believe it's genetic."

He grimaced. "Still, the first thought everyone will have is that I'm looking to weed out those people who have the condition. Everyone will be scared. Because this particular... illness sometimes remains unrecognized. For years. So even those who want the condition eradicated would be petrified that they might unknowingly be infected."

"If it's not genetic, it won't show up in a DNA test," she pointed out.

"Few valley people have been to college. They won't understand that detail."

He probably underestimated the locals. Lack of college did not necessarily mean 'dumb'. "Since you'd only test females of a certain age and—I assume—unmarried, couldn't you explain? If there's livestock breeding in this valley, surely they'd understand."

"And at least half the ladies would decide they should be my wife, despite the tests. It'd be like tossing a pig into a pool of hungry piranha. I doubt I would last as long as the pig."

"What an unflattering opinion you have of women." *Or an inflated opinion of himself.*

"When life doesn't offer many opportunities, people try to grab any that come along. Gender doesn't matter. Although—" He picked at unseen lint on his sleeve. "I will admit that Karen's sudden marriage to my father may have clouded my mind on the subject." He lowered his voice to a mutter. "Talk about inbred cows."

She had suspected this. If the valley's population had been isolated for a couple centuries, the genetic cohesion could be falling apart. "Purebred" dogs were often medical wrecks, while "mutts" were strong and healthy. Although livestock breeders often bred close relatives to emphasize certain characteristics, eventually, things fell apart.

"Won't it be the same, once I've finished? I mean, unless you plan to kidnap the woman and elope, then the valley will know you're looking for a bride."

"That's an interesting idea, eloping."

"I don't recommend it! Especially not by kidnapping!"

"Of course not." There was still a gleam in his eyes. "I just hadn't considered it before."

"I don't understand how you plan to do this. After I devise a list of, oh, let's say half a dozen, what then? If you start dating one, won't the other piranha start circling?"

"How astute. You're right. I'll have to move fast, send anonymous flowers, gifts, that sort of thing. Find a pretext to call, happen to run into her at the store, pause for a chat." His gaze was intense. "I can be done, if planned carefully. But as soon as people start to wonder, I'll have to sweep her off her feet and get engaged, before any piranha can get started."

He frowned thoughtfully. "An engagement won't necessarily stop them, though, so it will have to be a short one."

He acted as if every woman in the valley wanted to marry him.

Perhaps they did. The richest man they'd ever seen. Employer of virtually everyone they knew. Grand house with servants. Many considered that paradise. If the man professed adoration, that was gravy.

But he'd be lying to her, and that didn't sit well with Ondrea. By doing this family tree, she was assisting in that deception, and that sat even less well with her.

It's not my problem. This valley isn't my home. I don't know any of the women here, except Wilma, and Tarver's wife, Cook. Since both are married, this insane plan won't affect them. In the meantime, I have a job, and I'm getting paid well for it.

"You look very thoughtful," Morris commented.

Her eyes focused. "I was thinking that you've given this a lot of thought."

He hesitated. "Plans don't always go the way we expect." He opened the door and gestured her out. "And I never planned how you would entertain yourself. Perhaps you'd like to go into town for dinner and a movie next weekend."

Yes, she could afford that. Not every weekend, but this time, she could. "Thank you. When do you want Fredrick back? I wouldn't want to inconvenience either of you."

"Fredrick!" he repeated, and his mouth tightened. "Fredrick doesn't drive at night. It isn't safe to be out at night, even in a car."

"But you just suggested—"

"You're right," he said brusquely. "We'll make it a matinee and dinner. Slap lunch on the front, maybe a visit to the museum, and make it a full day. We'll consider it a date, then."

"A date!" She wasn't certain he'd actually meant that. "I don't date my employers."

He was silent until they entered the dining room. "Semantics," he decided. "I should have said, 'appointment', rather than 'date'. What that set your mind at ease?"

She nearly retorted that he could call it whatever he wanted, it was the intention that mattered. But she had made her feelings plain. She wanted to change the subject. "There's a museum in Morris Pointe?"

He smiled, held her chair for her. "A small one. It concentrates on this valley. History, flora, fauna, those types of things."

It offered something to do outside this house. Possibly even information that wasn't inside this house. "I'd like to visit that. How would I find it?"

"I couldn't send you to town without a guide. It's not set up on a grid, like most American cities. The streets wander, and I wouldn't risk you being lost."

His concern had become irritating. She had to work hard not to grind her teeth. "You feared I'd get lost in this house when I arrived."

"This house is made of straight lines. The streets of Morris Pointe are not." He waved her protest into silence. "Please humor me and accept a guide, this first time. After that—we'll see."

She'd humor him. One did sometimes need to trust the judgment of others.

* * *

Tarver helped Ondrea shrug her weighted coat on, then offered her scarf. The front door was open a crack as Morris waited outside for her, and cold seeped in insidiously. Ondrea buttoned her coat and tied the scarf around her head. "Have you gloves, Miss?" the butler asked.

"They're in my pocket," she said. *Among other things*. She reached for the door handle.

"Would you prefer coffee, tea or hot chocolate when you return?"

She stopped, surprised. She hadn't considered a hot drink to welcome her back. "Tea." Her hand was already cold, and she was indoors. "But I can't say how long we'll be."

"Not to worry, Miss. Cook will have it ready."

"Thank you, Tarver. And thank your wife, too." She stepped outside, into the deep shade cast over the porch.

Morris stood at the top of the steps, but he couldn't see the valley stretch before the house. The fog was still opaque. Ondrea felt tongue-tied when she stepped out, and stood uncertainly,

25

unwilling to disrupt his thoughts. The door closed silently, until the latch clicked.

Morris' head turned to face her, then his body followed suit as he looked her over. "You don't have boots or gloves?"

She shrugged, tried to adjust her coat, which drug on her shoulders. "My boots are in storage back home. I was under the impression spring had started when I was packing to come here." She had drawn her gloves from her coat pocket and now put them on.

"It probably had," he returned. "That's south and a lower altitude than here. Well, we'll stay on the walkways, so maybe boots aren't necessary. If nothing else, it looks like those shoes can be washed." He waved toward the north wing and they started in that direction along the top step, which became a walkway.

"I should have offered this before." He sounded apologetic. "All the other ladies have somebody they routinely ask, when they want or need to go outside."

"I's not a member of your household," she stated. She tried to keep her voice firm without making the statement a challenge. Sometimes an employer needed to be reminded of the boundaries between them. Having never lived in her employer's home before, she felt she needed to keep those boundaries in her own mind, as well.

"Never the less, I'm responsible for your well-being. Physical, mental... emotional."

"On the contrary, Mr Morris. my emotional health is not your concern. Likewise, I am capable of handling my own mental health. So, while I appreciate this walk, don't concern yourself with keeping me entertained. I'm sure you have more important things to occupy you."

He was quiet as they rounded the corner and started for the back. The ground was flat for several yards behind the house, where the garden was. Then the mountain started upward again.

"What about Friday?" he asked. "I eat lunch about 11:30, but then, we could walk in the garden again. Look for signs of spring. Assuming there isn't two feet of snow on the ground."

"Mr Morris—"

"Barry," he told her. "I will no longer call you Ms El Lobos if you will call me Barry."

It was tempting, since he hadn't managed to pronounce her name correctly even once. But he was her employer, and she had never called an employer by their given name. It could only lead to other, less innocent forms of familiarity. She continued the conversation without using any name. "I have work to do—"

"We went through this. Doc doesn't want you doing overtime," he broke in. "That leaves plenty of time for an occasional walk. The garden isn't large enough to take long."

She stared at the path they trod, as if unsure where to place her feet. They had reached the back corner, but instead of turning into the garden, Morris stopped, forcing her to stop also.

He raised her face. "Friday. Noon. A walk in the garden. Consider it an appointment."

"Is that an order, Mr Morris?" Despite her efforts, it came out hard and angry.

He shook his head, took a step closer. "No." His breath was welcome warmth on her face. "But if you feel guilty taking a respite, I can add it to your job description. 'Three times a week, walk in the garden and report on any changes noted.' Would that make it acceptable?"

It was the cold wind that made her lean forward, an attempt to find warmth in closeness. His eyes would normally be called ice blue, but to her, they were the blue of the tropical sky. Inside, a tingling heat began to spread, dispelling her anger and making her breathless, all at once. But her mind was numb, and it was hard to think. He seemed uncommonly close. Her heart was pumping hard, and the warmth spread, dispelling her goose bumps. She yearned to lose herself in the tropics.

"There you are."

The tropics slid away, and the arctic enveloped her in frigidity made worse by its unexpected contrast to ecstasy. She blinked and glanced around, recognized the Morris mansion, the beginning of the still-winter-bare garden.

Morris had his back to her, his coat stretched across tense shoulders. "Cooney."

Cooney stepped sideways to avoid a slush patch and caught sight of Ondrea. "Oh, she's emerged. Spring must be here."

"Doesn't feel like it," Ondrea muttered, hunkering down deep within her coat.

Morris asked, "Where have you been, Ralph? This time?"

"You heard the wolves, didn't you?" He waved vaguely up the mist-shrouded slope. "Some of them seemed close, so I looked for sign."

"Did you find any?"

"Nothing definite. A few scuff marks that could have been anything. Maybe the site of a rabbit kill about a mile away, but that's not definite."

Silence fell as clouds of vapor issued from their collective lungs. "Must have been a trick of mountain acoustics, to make them sound close. If you want lunch, you'd better get inside."

"Do you want me to take you to the possible rabbit kill?"

"Not today."

Cooney glanced at the overcast sky. "You might not be able to see anything tomorrow."

"According to you, you can't see anything definite today."

"Yes," Cooney agreed reluctantly. "I'll go eat, then." He set off toward the front of the house, his boots heavy on the flagstones.

Morris turned back to Ondrea, and gestured to the garden. "In another week, with luck, the men will start preparing the soil. With them here, you could come outside for a bit."

"Maybe," she allowed. "These are my only shoes half-way suitable for mud, and I don't want to wash them too often."

The entire back yard was garden. Morris pointed out various areas, each with its own bench, and explained which room would see that section, if the drapes were open. It would be lovely, once there was something besides bare limbs and mud.

Outside her office were roses, beds for irises and daisies, and a lilac bush. Ondrea got as close to the office windows as the flagstone path would let her, and tried to imagine what her view would be like in a few weeks. Her eyes immediately landed on the lilac bush, which she had last seen shrouded in mist. She shivered.

"Cold?"

She felt foolish. "When the wolves howled, I imagined one might be behind that lilac. Silly, of course." The fog had retreated beyond the bush, barely blurred the slope behind it.

"Sure," Morris agreed, but started in that direction.

Her heart in her throat, Ondrea followed him around the bush. There was no wolf, of course, but when Morris stepped off the path and bent to examine the ground, her lungs refused to work. She could barely ask, "What is it?"

"Dog tracks," he stated, and returned to the path.

"Are you sure? Dog and wolf tracks are much the same."

"I can tell," he answered easily.

She stared at the depression. Even at this distance, it looked too big, even for his dogs.

"Just a dog print," he repeated. "No doubt one of the dogs made a pit stop here." His hand on her elbow guided her away. "Now, over here, lilies of the valley surround this fountain. If you look closely, you can see the first leaves peeking through the mud."

They moved on, through the garden, ever closer to going inside again, into the warmth.

As they approached the south end of the garden, which Ondrea imagined was behind the kitchen, a big man approached with two of the huge dogs. Ondrea stopped, swallowed and reminded her escort, "I don't like dogs."

Morris frowned. "I very much want to talk to Vernon."

"Point me to the nearest door, and I'll go inside," she offered.

"It'd be a shame to cut your outing short," he muttered, and pointed to a bench under a nearby tree. "Sit there a minute. I won't be long." As she moved toward the bench, he met the approaching dogs and their handler.

The stone bench looked cold, and Ondrea's toes were already numb. She tried to keep from freezing by pacing in front of the bench; four steps one way, turn around, four steps back.

During her pacing, Ondrea glimpsed a cave in the slope, set back from the garden, with vines writhing around the edges. When the vines were in full leaf, it would be all but impossible to see this cave entrance. Flagstones led to it, but a pair of benches made it seem like the path was only there to facilitate reaching a seat.

The men's conversation faded as Ondrea stepped toward the vine-choked cave. The entrance beckoned, promised a cease to all her problems, if she stepped inside. Reaching the last flagstone, she tried to look inside, but it was pitch dark. It might as well have been solidified blackness. *If I step inside, my eyes could adjust, and—*

Something grabbed her wrist, jerked her back into dim daylight. "Don't go in there!" Morris' breath was a warm fog around her that, unfortunately, did nothing to thaw the ice her nose had become. "What were you thinking?"

"I wanted to know what was inside," she returned, and slipped from his grasp, breathed into her cupped hands, trying to warm her face.

"Not your business!" His hand was an iron claw digging into her arm as he jerked her toward the house. His long strides and unrelenting grip made her trot to keep from being drug. He opened a French door, shoved the drape away, and they were in the dining room. By the time Morris slammed and locked the door, Tarver entered with the promised goodies.

"None for me!" Morris growled, and stomped down the hall.

"He seems out of sorts," Tarver intoned. "The full moon's approach does that to him."

The butler was trying to tell her something, but Ondrea couldn't imagine what. And she didn't think to ask until he had left the room, leave a mug of hot tea and a plate of warm cookies to help thaw her half-frozen body.

* * *

There was a diary laying on her desk when Ondrea returned to her office. It hadn't been there when she left. Who could have left it for her. Morris? No, he had been with her.

The diary had been written by Phillip Morris in 2006. Probably the father of the current Mr Morris, or some uncle or cousin. It held a series of book marks. She opened the book to the first piece of torn paper and sat down to read.

From the diary of Phillip Morris, January 8, 2006:

I received a visit this afternoon from Karen Reynolds, a pretty girl about Barry's age. I assumed she wanted Barry, who was out. She pouted, said she had talked to Barry, but he refused to listen. Therefore, she had come to me.

She had dated Barry. He had mentioned a Karen a few times, but not recently. She claimed Barry got her pregnant, and that he refused to make her "an honest woman". I didn't realize anybody used that phrase anymore.

The strangest part was my reaction. I believed every word she said, thought her the most beautiful woman I'd ever seen! I promised to do anything I could. She kissed me, and I suddenly had an erection! Though I haven't thought of another woman since my darling Jane died.

After she left, I puzzled over what had happened. When Barry returned, I asked if he'd seen Karen lately. His response was, "Who?" Obviously, she hasn't been on his mind. If Barry got her pregnant, it would be on his mind.

Now I don't believe a word she said, though I remember how I felt while she was here.

I begin to understand, I think, how early settler wives were 'seduced' by Noah Silas. Myth says those cursed can exert this influence over the opposite gender. I had thought it an excuse, but I begin to believe it may be true.

Ondrea paused, as confused by the entry as the man who had written it. The girl had wanted the father to make the son marry her. That was clear. Had Barry been too stubborn? The father had married her, so that the child had a name. Stranger things had been known.

She turned to the next piece of paper.

From the diary of Phillips Morris — June 9, 2006:

I married her. Despite my instructions what I wasn't to be alone in her presence, my determination to have nothing to do with her. I remember the ceremony. Vaguely. I don't remember how she got me to the east slope chapel, but I do remember the ceremony.

I have locked myself in my room. The marriage will not be consummated.

Barry is scheduled to start university this fall. I will have Fredrick drive him there tomorrow, help him get 'settled in'.

The servants have instructions; all males will always have a female working with them. I've already seen her make eyes at young Ralph Cooney, and the ink isn't dry on our marriage certificate! A bitch in heat.

Karen isn't smart enough to do this.

What a strange ending to the entry. The whole entry, really, didn't make any sense. Why get married, if he wasn't willing? Such used to happen, but it was usually the woman whose willingness wasn't necessary.

Ondrea went to the library and found the Legal Log of 2006, found the marriage license for Phillip Morris and Karen Reynolds. Karen's signature was an indecipherable scrawl. Morris' was careful and methodical, a copperplate signature.

Frowning, Ondrea took the Legal Log to her office and compared Morris' signature on the marriage license to the writing in his diary. The letters had the same form, but the signature seemed to have required more thought. As if he had concentrated on each letter, one at a time. Most people didn't have to think about signing their name.

Could Morris have been drugged? She turned back to the journal.

From the diary of Phillip Morris — October 7, 2006:

Yancy Zelany died last night.

I took the men hunting, since the moon was full. We

were successful, for once, and trudged home in the wee hours, somber and grim. We seldom manage to kill one of Them. When we do, it always affects us deeply.

As we paused in the entrance hall, uncertain what to do with the body, Karen appeared, her robe barely fastened, and belittled our hunting skills. Cooney was at the top of the stairs, half dressed.

I had the body brought in. As Yancy sprawled on the floor, his cold, naked body still showing patches of fur and a stump of a tail, Karen stared in shock. Cooney turned away, headed for his own bed for a change, I think.

Probably too late for him.

It was small of me to do it that way, I suppose. But satisfying. Karen seems different. Uncertain. As if she's lost her direction.

I'll have to tell Yancy's wife myself. It won't be easy.

Ondrea sat in shock for a moment. The Morris' hunted <u>people</u>? She was suddenly very thankful Dr Jad had insisted she bring guns. There was danger in this valley; he had been right about that. But it wasn't the wolves that were dangerous.

That entry could not say what it seemed to. She turned to the Legal Log, found Yancy Zelany's death certificate. Died of multiple gunshot wounds received in a hunting accident. That seemed straight-forward enough. But how many 'hunting accidents' had there been over the past two centuries?

There was one more piece of paper designating another diary entry.

From the diary of Phillip Morris — December 5, 2006:

She's corrupted Cooney. I'm not surprised. He always was a bit wild. But these days, the dogs can't stand him. Not a good sign.

Tonight is a full moon. Two have been seen in this vicinity several times.

Keep your friends close, and your enemies even

closer. But there's such a thing as being too close. I want to end this tonight.

He sounded like any cuckolded husband out for revenge. And yet, he didn't like Karen. It didn't make any sense.

The remaining pages were blank. That had been his final entry.

Ondrea turned to the Legal Log again, found the death certificates for Karen and Phillip Morris. She had died of multiple gunshot wounds. He had been torn apart by wolves.

Ondrea's hands shook as she set the books aside. The insinuations in them couldn't be real. Somebody was playing a joke on her. Cooney, probably. She couldn't prove it, of course.

She went back to the library, selected a diary at random, opened it in the middle. She needed ordinary, everyday events to calm her nerves.

From the diary of Clara Long Silas, July 28, 1904:

> *We tested the baby last night. I was a full moon, so we put her cradle in front of the window, and stayed up all night as the moonlight washed over her.*
>
> *Everybody says children are exempt, but everybody tests their baby at the first full moon. She remained our sweet baby all night, and we wept in relief.*
>
> *We named her Gloria.*

Ondrea's inclination was to find the birth certificate for Gloria, but she didn't. She had wanted ordinary and everyday, but had gotten drama and innuendo. Time to stop for the day.

She shut down the computer, stacked the books on her desk. As she stepped into the hallway, she heard music; old-fashioned, scratchy movie music, it seemed.

On the other side of the corridor, between her and the foyer, she heard the music leaking out a door that stood ajar. She peeked in, expecting to find someone watching TV. What she found was a home theater. A huge screen dominated one wall, faced by several comfortable love seats. The back wall was covered in shelves, nearly full of videos.

The room was empty, but a black and white image of a foggy field showed on the screen. With a dramatic blare of music, the title came on: Wolf Man! "Oh, good grief," Ondrea muttered, again wondering who was trying to warn her. Or scare her.

She went to the central hallway, and then hesitated, wondering what to do. She needed to calm down, and get her mind off the absurdity of what had been implied. She retreated to her room for some Tai Chi. And if that didn't work, she'd finish the afternoon with daytime TV. That was pretty mind-numbing.

*   *   *

Ondrea was surprised to enter the small dining room and find only one setting on the table. Wilma entered with her salad and bread, and it became obvious she was expected to eat alone tonight. "Isn't Mr Morris joining me tonight?"

"He's gone out, Miss." There was the slightest quiver in the maid's voice. Fear, uncertainty or nervousness. It was impossible to tell which. But the set of her mouth said that was all she was going to say on the subject.

For the first time, Ondrea ate dinner alone. The conversation was definitely lacking.

*   *   *

Ondrea sat bolt upright in her bed. Her eyes frantically searched her dark bedroom for whatever had awakened her. Moonlight made blurry puddles of light below each window. It was the only thing in her room that hadn't been there when she had climbed into bed.

A dull roar sounded outside, almost too distant to be heard. Morris was hunting! Her heart hammering, she inched out of bed to stare out the window, but nothing moved. She jumped at the sound of another gunshot, and couldn't catch her breath for some time.

35

Enough. This was insane. She couldn't take any more.

*   *   *

Ondrea lifted her head from the banister support and opened her eyes to find Morris standing halfway up the staircase, staring at her. His boots and jeans were covered in mud. "What are you doing up?"

She carefully straightened stiff joints and climbed to her feet at the top of the staircase to face him with as much calm assurance as she could muster. "I want Fredrick to take me to Morris Pointe. I'm returning to university."

He grunted and stared at her, his eyes narrowed. "Done with your work already?"

"I'm not finishing the work. It's too dangerous for me to stay here."

He scowled, and started up the remainder of the steps. "Well, you have to."

She stared at him in shock. "You're keeping me prisoner?" The words were out before she had thought things through.

He had reached the top of the stairs, and stood staring at her, his brow lowered. There were dark smudges under his eyes, and his tropical eyes were grayed with storm clouds. His face was drawn and pinched, his shoulders rounded with fatigue. If she hadn't known what he'd been doing all night, she'd reach out to offer him comfort.

"Not me." His gravel voice pulled her back to her accusation. "Nature. Melting snow has made the bridge impassible. We'll have to wait a few days for the water to go down."

He turned away from her, headed down the north ring. She thought of following, then thought better of it. What was the use? How could she argue with a swollen river and a flooded bridge? Unshed tears burned her eyes as she returned to her room.

*   *   *

36

Ondrea looked up from her computer screen to the window to rest her eyes. The weather had remained the same; cold and foggy. For days. She'd always imagined England was like this. But this wasn't England.

The fog pressed against the window panes gave her nothing to focus her eyes on. She let them roam around the office instead.

There was a stack of books on her desk. She found one every morning, with bits of paper for bookmarks. She refused to look in them until she came to them in the course of her work.

So they sat, beckoning but ignored. Mysterious. Creepy.

This whole place had gotten creepy. Reading material left on her desk. Flowers, perfume and other gifts left in her room, tied up with pretty ribbons, but never giving a clue who had left it. So she didn't know who to thank, who to give them back to.

Her door opened. She turned to find Morris leaning against the door jamb, still tired but no longer muddy. It's 11:30," he observed. She glanced at her watch and nodded in confirmation. "It's Friday," he went on.

His behavior was confusing. "Is it? I guess I lost track."

His brows lowered. "The garden isn't buried in snow. Yet."

"That is surprising." She wondered what he was trying to say.

He sighed in exasperation. "You didn't put it in your appointment book, did you?"

"What appointment—?" A memory clicked into place. "You didn't mean that, did you?"

"I said it was an appointment. Come on, let's have lunch."

She didn't want to. Cooney was amused by how quiet and subdued, tense, dinner had become since Morris had lost his temper in the garden. Now Morris expected her to repeat the whole thing. She didn't want to.

She sighed and stood up to have lunch.

* * *

The garden was the same. There hadn't been enough sun to help things grow, because of the fog. Cold temperatures hadn't

37

helped. They strolled from one end to the other, retracing their steps from the earlier visit, minus the circle around the bush.

And minus the talk. Neither made any effort to introduce words into the situation.

Nature made up for their lapse with faint rolls of thunder, chiding them for intruding into its domain. Or else urging them to forgive and forget, for they were both human, after all.

At long last, they reached the south end of the garden, and paused beneath the tree with the bench. Ondrea turned her back to the cave, the source of Morris' earlier anger. She wondered why he had stopped here, then saw the big man, Vernon, approaching them. This time, he didn't have any dogs with him.

Morris cleared his throat. "That's the cave that interested you last time."

"I know. You don't want me going in there."

"I don't think you'll want to go in, once you find out what it is."

"That sounds cryptic."

His mouth curled, his blue eyes glinted despite the fog. "What a serendipity choice of words. Because that cave is the family crypt."

A deafening crack of thunder shook them to the core, and hailstones pelted down. Morris grabbed her arm, and shoved her into the black cave. Suddenly blind, her ears still ringing, Ondrea clutched to him, afraid she'd be left alone in the unknown darkness.

"Hang on," Morris whispered. "Guess we're stuck here for a while."

"Well, we've been expecting this for days, huh?" Asked another voice. The black bulk that blocked the entrance must be Vernon.

A light flared suddenly, aimed at the stone ceiling, which was only a couple feet above their heads. The flashlight was passed to Vernon, and Morris pulled two more from the shelf. In half a second, he pressed a flashlight into Ondrea's hands.

"You're in after all. I'd prefer to just wait for the hail to stop, but I don't suppose that will happen." He aimed his light into the cave, revealing stone boxes hugging the left wall.

Ondrea had had a strong urge to explore when it was a hole into the mountain. Knowing what it was, she wanted to leave. The clatter of hail on the garden flagstones said she couldn't.

"Have you ever been to a cemetery?" Vernon asked. "That's all this is, really. Just seems spookier because it's dark, I suppose."

"We're underground," Morris added. "Kind of like we're buried, too."

"Now, there's a morbid sense of humor," Vernon said.

"No, he's right," Ondrea decided, and swallowed the lump in her throat. "It's just a cemetery that seems spooky because we're underground with the bodies. But they can't hurt us. So there's no reason to be frightened."

"Very logical." Morris' voice was deep and rumbly, like thunder echoing through the underworld. "Some people like cemeteries, like to look at dates and names, imagine what life was like for this woman or that man."

His flashlight played over the boxes. "I know the names of those who rest here. Their blood is in my veins, and the happenings of their lifetimes, their thoughts, are in their diaries."

"Genealogy," Ondrea muttered. It wasn't any warmer here than outside. "Do hailstorms last long here?" Ondrea asked.

"Not usually. Why?"

"I have to keep moving, or my feet will freeze." She stamped her feet, trying to chase the numbness away. "We might as well look at names and dates, just to keep moving."

Morris sighed. "If you insist."

"Isn't this why you wanted me to meet you?" Vernon asked.

They had something planned. Ondrea tried to read their faces, but it was too dark, behind the flashlight bulbs, to see much of anything. She hadn't expected anything during the day, but she was glad— A hand crept into her pocket, reassured her that the gun was present, though the weight dragging on her shoulders should have told her.

"I hope it's not too soon." Ondrea wondered what Morris meant by that as he moved deeper inside. He waited by the first stone box, his light low, so they could see where to walk.

Ondrea moved forward, played her light over the inscription. "Dalton Morris. Died October 11, 1844."

"The original Morris in this valley. My several-times-great grandfather. The next is his wife, who only survived him by two days."

Ondrea stepped closer. "Helen Cooney Morris." She turned. "She was a Cooney?"

"I told you, I'm related to everybody in this valley."

"Except Ms Ellobos," Vernon stated.

"Well, and I'm only related to the dogs by marriage." Both men laughed, but they were tight, forced laughs.

Never-the-less, their joke dispelled the last hard edge of awkwardness from their situation. They continued. Morris always had some comment to make about each person, knowledge of some quirk of that individual, or a statement about the times they lived through. They approached the end of the coffins.

"Jane Nichols Morris," Ondrea read, and the dates.

"My mother," Barry Morris stated flatly.

"Oh." The briefest moment of arithmetic told Ondrea that he was 29, or thereabouts. She had thought him older.

His hand was not as cold as hers. She pondered the difference as his hand covered hers, directed the flashlight to the next inscription. "Phillip Morris, my father." He released the light, stepped to the last coffin. "That brings us to Karen Reynolds Morris, my step-mother."

Ondrea swept her light that way, gasped, and stepped back in shock, running into the huge bulk of the hired hand. Karen's coffin was open!

Vernon's big hands wrapped around her arms. "She can't hurt you," he stated softly.

"Why is hers open?" Ondrea's voice was unsteady.

"Have you read the diaries?" Morris asked.

She wondered if he meant the specific diaries left on her desk, or all the diaries gathered in the library. There was no way she could have read all the diaries already. "Some of them."

"Have you figured it out yet? What the Morris Valley Wolves are?"

She shook her head slowly. "You can't be serious."

He gazed into the open casket. "If it's not true, then Karen's skeleton is normal."

Silence fell, so deep even their breathing seemed hushed. What a strange tableau they made in the sparse light. Ondrea mused. Tall and handsome Morris staring into his lost love's coffin, while his henchman held her—the bemused outsider—a prisoner.

That wasn't fair, wasn't accurate. She may be bemused, but she wasn't a prisoner. Vernon's hand wasn't a vice on her arm; it offered support, as did his body. She was the one leaning against him, her knees too weak to support her.

"Have you ever seen a skeleton, Ondrea?" Morris asked quietly.

"Some. Mostly to compare human with animal. A lot of the bones serve the same purpose, but they're shaped different."

"Exactly," he agreed, and his tropics gaze rose to her face. "I won't make you look. We can leave, if you want. And if the hail has stopped. But it is just a skeleton. Just bones."

She raised her chin. He thought she was afraid. She had been surprised, but that was all. "What if I see a normal human skeleton?"

"Then, obviously, my father brainwashed me."

She pressed her lips together and found her strength, walked forward to stand beside him. She swallowed and aimed her flashlight inside. There was still bright yellow hair around the perfectly human skull. White fabric hid the torso, but the hands had long, normal finger bones.

The dress was less than knee length. Karen would have preferred short dresses. The leg bones were... misshaped. The foot bones were twice as long as they should have been.

How could she have walked, with feet like that?

Ondrea carefully moved the skirt aside, grunted to find the thigh bones too short for a human. She moved more fabric aside, sure the perpetrators of this horrible joke had placed a wolf's hindquarters at the base of the human torso.

She was wrong. The wolf thighs were properly inserted into

the sockets of a strangely deformed wolf pelvis. The pelvis, in fact, was too malformed to be either a wolf's or a human's, while the spine was plainly human. Underneath was a blond wolf tail.

"She—" She could hardly get the acknowledgement out. "She was a werewolf."

Morris moved up, put the dress back in place. "One of the Morris Valley Wolves." His words warmed the side of her face, fluttered wisps of hair that had escaped her braid. "When they're shot, it breaks their concentration, or something, and they start the transformation back to human. If they die quickly—and you'd better hope they do—they don't complete the transformation. They remain something in-between."

His hand covered hers. She shivered as he gently turned her away. "The hail should have stopped by now. I think we'll all be glad to get inside to warm cookies and hot drinks."

"I think a steaming bubble bath might be the only way to soak the chill out of me." Or maybe something else. It probably wasn't the temperature that had her frozen. Not anymore.

Morris grunted and took a step toward the entrance. "I was thinking the same thing."

Her steps were uncertain. She was glad for Morris at her side, for Vernon waiting, ready to take a supporting place on her other side. Her flashlight shone haphazardly, its beam quivering because the hand that held it trembled.

She stopped in surprise as her light glinted off something between two coffins. "What's that?" She steadied the beam on the inscriptions, to be sure of her location.

"She's found it," Vernon muttered.

"It was too much to hope she wouldn't. She's observant."

"What did I find?" There had been other small caskets, children who had not survived into adulthood, or even childhood. But those had been in line with the others.

This coffin lay against the wall, half hidden by his parents' coffins. The space between them was unusually small, making it almost impossible to approach the child's resting place.

Somehow, Ondrea managed to pick out the name. "Suzanne Xylia Morris."

"Obviously, you haven't come to her yet in your studies," Morris said. "My sister.

Ondrea couldn't see his face in the dimness. "You said she was stolen at three."

"That's what my father told people. Only three of us knew the truth, and dad's dead."

She pondered that a moment. "Death isn't easy to accept, especially for a parent. He might have been in denial. Perhaps her being stolen was preferable to her being dead."

"No," he stated. "Not in denial. Her being stolen was preferable to how she had died."

She didn't know what to say. Her head whirled. "You know that I'm not your sister?"

"What?" He sounded surprised. "Of course you're not. Why would I think you were?"

"Well, Cooney—"

"Oh." He shifted his weight to the other leg. "Knew he was up to something. Still don't know what." He cleared his throat. "I helped dad construct Suzanne's resting place. He knew what was what. His over-riding concern was that they would not win."

Why did people only explain thing half way? "Who wouldn't win what?"

"Think she's ready to hear the whole thing?" Vernon asked softly.

Morris shuddered. "No." He turned to leave.

"Well, tell me something!" Ondrea demanded. "Lie to me, if you mush! Otherwise, I'll stew about it, and what I imagine will undoubtedly be far worse than the truth!"

He hesitated, but didn't look t her. "The wolves, Ms El Lobos," he said at last. "Dad was determined the wolves would not take over the valley." He trudged forward. "Now come along. The weather has turned to snow, and we all need to warm up.

Ondrea followed, her flashlight aimed down so she wouldn't trip on uneven flooring. She had invited him to lie, but she couldn't decide if he had.

The day was still dim when they reached the crypt's mouth. Snow swirled out of the fog and was already collecting around the bit of ice that nearly covered the flagstones. They returned the flashlights to the shelf, hunkered down into their coats, and ventured out.

By the time Ondrea was halfway to the tree, Morris' form had become fuzzy by thickening fog and fat snowflakes. Vernon, behind her, had already caught her twice when her feet had slipped. He hadn't forgotten her, even if his employer had.

She heard a muffled sound, and staggered as Vernon's bulk bumped against her. Her arms flew out to either side as she tried to stay upright. "Vernon? You okay?" He didn't answer, just grabbed her arms and threw her to the ground.

Her chest hurt, the air knocked from her. Her cheek burned, scraped by the flagstone and frozen by hail and snow. Somebody—more than one—held her down, heavy weights bearing down on her shoulders. Someone else fussed with her long coat, shoved the hem up to her waist.

"What are you doing?"

Someone laughed, low and throaty. "Just let it happen, and you won't be hurt. Much."

Let it happen? What have they done to Vernon? Where's Morris?

The coat was shoved up around her waist. It couldn't be pushed any further, for her upper body was still held down. Someone began tugging at her slacks, tried to pull them down. There was no mistaking their intention.

Her hands were free, though their motion was restricted. She fumbled for her pockets. Dr Jad hadn't known exactly what she'd find in Morris Valley, but she wasn't unprotected.

Her slacks tore. Goose bumps rose on her buttocks. The fabric was ripped away in big gobs. Where were her pockets?

"Ondrea?" Morris sounded breathless. In pain, possibly. "Vernon?"

"Boss." Vernon sounded even weaker, disorientated.

"Barry! Hel—" Something hit her head, scraping her cheek across the flagstone again.

"Kill him." She knew that voice! "Kill them both. We only need her. The long-lost sister. And she will be one of us." Strong hands positioned her hips and knees.

"Ralph, I'm not his sister!"

"Of course not," Ralph agreed. "His sister's dead. Killed during one of their full moon hunts as she learned what Yancy had made her. The only juvenile we've ever taken."

"Stop yapping, Ralph!" one of Ondrea's captors snapped. It might have been a woman. "Change and take her! Others'll come looking for them soon!"

"But if the sister's dead, then I can't be her!"

"Nobody knows little Suzanne is dead except the two men who were there when it happened. And us. Old man Morris is dead. Vernon soon will be. And we ain't telling."

"Damn it, Ralph, do it! We won't get another opportunity like this!"

"I'd rather enjoy her as a man first.!"

"We don't have time!"

Ondrea finally found her left coat pocket, and wriggled her hand inside, wrapped it around the handle. Ralph's hands caressed her nether regions, which made her stomach churn.

She heard sounds of fighting, some from the direction of the cave, some from the area of the tree. How many of these creatures were there?

"Alright." Ralph's voice was harsh and low. "Give me a minute, and I'll get this done."

Her right hand snagged the other pocket's edge, lost it again.

She didn't bother to pull the left gun out, hardly tried to aim. She just twisted her wrist so the barrel was pointed more or less where she wanted, and pulled the trigger. The creature, person, whatever, on that side yipped and their grip loosened.

Ondrea twisted toward her back, kicking fiercely. As her rump rolled toward the ground, she pointed the gun behind her and shot again, hoping she didn't hit her own feet. Talons dug into her right shoulder to hold her still. She tried to twist the gun in that direction, but the bulk of the coat got in the way

Her right hand finally slipped into her other pocket. She kicked and wriggled, twisted and slid, trying to escape or at least get her gun pointed at something again.

Noise was everywhere. Yips and yaps. Voices yelling. Dogs barking and wolves growling. Guns blasting.

"Ondrea!"

"Here!" she yelled, and kicked something away that was pawing at her legs. She got her hand around the right gun and shot at whatever still held that shoulders.

The talons dug deeper. "Missed, bitch. Ralph, hurry up!"

Something grunted behind her, and claws scratched her legs trying to force them apart. She tried to ignore the pain in her shoulder, her face, her legs— Tried to ignore all her pain and discharged both guns in Ralph's direction.

How many times had she shot? How many bullets did she have left?

"Irene Silas." Barry suddenly loomed, looking in disgust at the old woman holding down her shoulder. A horrendous boom silenced the world, and wetness spattered Ondrea's face. The talons in her shoulder loosened their grip, slipped away.

Ondrea kicked and scooted over the stones, saw another flash from Barry's shotgun, felt her back ram into a bench leg. She pulled her handguns from her pockets, tried to straighten the tatters of her coat to hide as much of her nakedness as she could.

First, her hearing began to return. More shots and shouts rang in the fog, some close, some father away. Then, the bedlam began to fade. Voices still called to one another, but they seemed to be human voices, calling names.

Ondrea was trembling so badly she couldn't possibly climb to her feet and head for the house. All she could do was wait. Try not to cry. Try not to think about what had happened. What might still happen, if—

"Ondrea?"

Her guns jerked up. They were visibly shaking, but they were up, pointed at the dark shapes she could barely see in the fog and snow. "Who is it?"

"Barry." He started forward.

"Don't come any closer!" she warned. Her hearing still wasn't back to normal. How could she be sure it was him? Or of anything? This whole situation was impossible.

The dim form had stopped. Snow gathered in her lap, to match the ice and snow beneath her. The fog was brighter, possibly thinner. "Well, this sure wasn't what I had in mind for today's appointment," he said. "I hope tomorrow's goes better."

It sounded like him. She licked her lips, spat out blood and mud that her tongue picked up. "What's tomorrow's appointment?"

"Is she—" Another figure moved up, was stopped by the first. "She's armed. Her nerves are raw. Better let me handle this."

"What's tomorrow's appointment?" she repeated, her teeth gritted.

He took a small step forward. The fog had thinned; she was beginning to discern features—two eyes, a nose and mouth. Blue eyes. She longed for the tropical sky.

"A trip into town," he answered. "A visit to the museum, lunch, a matinee and dinner. That's what we settled on, wasn't it?"

"I'll need a guide," she mumbled.

"You are my only appointment for the whole day," he answered.

She gave one short, hard nod. For an appointment, it sure sounded like a date.

Her cheek was on fire. Her naked butt was frozen from sitting on the flagstones, snow and hail. Her legs were bleeding, her shoulders ached. Sometimes, you had to trust someone, do something. She struggled to her feet, turned to the house. "I need a bath."

"Tarver!" Morris barked.

"I'll have Wilma start the water, sir."

* * *

Ondrea sat on the chaise lounge with her bathrobe pulled tight and looked out the window at the moon-drenched valley below.

Cook and Wilma had tended her wounds, even before she got to bathe. The side of her face was scraped badly. She might be scarred for life. She could hardly raise her arms. The scratches on

47

her legs were deep, held closed by tape right now. She might need stitches.

If she lived until morning.

Barry sat down, wrapped one arm around her and handed her a goblet. Warmth soaked into her fingers and she smelled spices on the wine's steam. "When you said hot drink, I imagined hot cocoa," she muttered, and sipped gratefully.

"I thought you needed something stronger."

"Yeah, it isn't every day a woman gets raped. Let alone by a werewolf."

His arm tightened, making her wince. He glanced at the three men sitting along the wall, their guns loaded, and spares at hand. "Did he? Rape you?"

"No." She pushed blurred memories away and sighed. "I don't think so."

"That's how the curse is passed along," he explained. "Sex with a werewolf while he or she is in wolf form."

She drank deeply. "But he said your sister—"

"Pedophilia," he choked out.

She thought she might throw up. "Poor Suzanne."

"They want to rule the valley, and if one of them lives in this house, that becomes easier." He looked thoughtful for a moment. "At this point, we don't know if any of them got away today. Or if there were some who didn't come."

It was a sobering thought. Ondrea drank the rest of her wine.

Moonlight fell in a patch on the floor, crept closer. Ondrea was tired. She wanted this over, one way or the other. She put her head in Barry's lap and lay down. Although her toes reached the end of the chaise, there were several inches to go before the moonlight touched her.

"Is this too soon? Will the test work? It's only been a few hours."

He smoothed her hair. The tropical sky was grayed. "I don't know."

"If nothing happens, we'd better do it again tomorrow night. Maybe next month, too."

He swallowed. "We'll have to."

She tried to keep the tears from gathering, tried to figure out what else to say. "Barry—"

"I know."

Her mouth worked futilely for a time before she finally gave up. "I'm going to sleep," she told him at last. "If I— Then I don't want to know about it."

She closed her eyes, refusing to look at those three men and their guns. Liquid escaped her eyes, burned as it soaked her bandage. Her head was swimming. From the wine, she hoped. She willed her eyes to stay closed, her breathing to slow.

She had determinedly held him at arm's length in the few days she'd been here, but during the nights, she had dreamt of wrapping her arms around him, of his warm hands caressing her body. His kisses would—

A light pressure on her mouth made half her face hurt. "Ow."

Barry grunted. "Well, that's a novel reaction to my kiss."

No, no, she wanted to sleep through it. Or at least pretend she was sleeping. "Don't wake me up!" she pled.

"Time to get dressed. I want to go to the hospital and get you checked out by a doctor before we start that appointment."

Her eyes flew open. The room was bright, sunlight streamed through the window. The armed men had disappeared as completely as the night. "I'm alive?"

"You were completely awash in moonlight, and all you did was snore."

She was afraid to hope. "Well— It wasn't really a full moon."

He frowned, unwilling not to hope. "Full enough. Now, are you going to get dressed or not?" She sat up and adjusted her robe. "About that appointment we have today."

Her head jerked up. "What about it?"

"Can we stop play-acting and call it a date? Cause that's sure what I mean for it to be."

She started to throw her arms around his neck, but her shoulders were too stiff. She pressed herself against him. "Come to think of it, didn't you say the bridge was out?"

He cleared his throat, and when she looked up, his face had turned pink. "I couldn't just let you leave, walk out of my life. Not when—" He took a deep breath. "There's another stop I'd like to make while we're in town."

"Before or after the hospital?"

"After. City Hall. For a marriage license." For a long moment, she couldn't move, couldn't breathe, couldn't think. "As soon as you pass the test next month, I want to get married."

"You'll protect me from the piranha?"

He laughed. "Happily, but I think the piranha haven't got a chance against you. Not if you're armed." He gave her a long hug, then sighed and let her go. "You'd better get some clothes on, or we might not make it into town at all. And not because the bridge is out." He got up and started for the door, paused to look back. "Not that I'd object to that kind of date." With a smirk, he left the room.

Neither would I. She smiled as she got to her feet. Based on his actions these past few days, that would come soon enough.

The End

Romance by Linda (NMI) Joy

The Secret in Morris Valley - Ondrea is sent to Morris Valley to study the wolves, but Barry Morris won't let her out of the house without a heavily armed guard. He has plans for Ondrea. So do the wolves. (60 pages)

The Game - (E-book only.) In the tiny town of Belgrade, 4 cousins have been raised more like brothers, each trying to out-do the others all the way through high school. One night when the eldest is back in town, visiting from college, their relationship is torn apart by revelations made by two of them. (24 pages.)

Hank's Widow - She wanted a quiet place to pursue her writing. He's loved her since he first saw her photo. Will her grief prevent him from claiming her heart? (340 pages.)

Boxed Set - The Game & Hank's Widow - (E-book only.) Get both "The Game" and <u>Hank's Widow</u> in a 'boxed set' for one low price.

Waiting for Glori - (Tentatively scheduled for 2022.) She finally escaped her husband. Now she must grow up and become self-sustaininng. How long will it take her to realize love is still available?

Fantasy by Trudy V Myers

The Atlans: The Truth/The Legend - The Atlans claim to be descended from Gods. The legend isn't far from the truth. (E-book only.)

The Woman on the Dock - When an Atlan warrior finds a woman tied to the dock as a direct provocation, she must decide how best to react. (E-book only.)

The Cave - A cave can supply shelter from a coming storm, or danger from creatures that have also sought shelter. This cave, it turns out, offers much more. (E-book only.)

Hero - Herotio grew up hearing tales of the adventures of various heroes of old. He finds out early that being a hero isn't as easy as it sounds. (E-book only.)

Cali - (currently available only in print) Cali has been left for dead—twice—by a gang of men who also killed 2 children left in her care. Sidek tags along as she searches for those men, wondering if there'll be any pieces to pick up if she finds them again. (240 pages.)

Science Fiction by John Lars Shoberg

The Stone Builders - An accident in the forest uncovers a hidden underground city left by previous colonists. Everything in the city is built of stone. Can the scientists discover what chased these previous colonists away before the same thing happens to them? (273 pages.)

The Waste Gun - Dr Von Scorio has developed a way to permanently dispose of radioactive waste. Others see it as a threat to the Earth. (247 page.)

De-Evolution - Two colony children lost in a violent storm leads to first contact with a sentient native race, and a mystery that must be solved if the colony is to survive.

The Stone Ship - (The Stone Builders #2) The military finds a derelict piece of a spaceship made of stone and reassemble the team that studied the stone artifacts before. Can they figure out what happened before the ship currently bearing down on them gets there? Is it the Stone Builders? Or whatever race cut the stone ship in half? (263 pages.)

And the Meek Shall Inherit... - The Lankmerans are a peacful civilization; they've never had any war in their history. Shortly after the human arrive, another species does also, and their intentions are NOT friendly! If the humans can't protect the Lankmerans, their entire race will be exterminated. And Earth may be be the next target for these single-minded invaders.

About MoonPhaze:

MoonPhaze started as a very small publishing company. But our authors are into more than writing; they like to cosplay as well as practice various hobbies.

You are invited to visit

www.MoonPhaze.com

where you can purchase copies of our paperback books,

browse our collection of cosplay prosthetics and other items,

visit our author's pages, and

see where we'll be making personal appearances.

Hope to see you there!